A
BIG
COLLECTION
of
Little
Golden Books®

Introduction by Kate Klimo

Contents

Introduction

In *Citizen Kane,* Orson Welles's epic cinematic masterpiece, Charles Foster Kane is possessed by a childhood memory of a little wooden sled on which was painted the name "Rosebud." For millions of Americans, Little Golden Books represent a vast and flourishing garden of "rosebuds," the warm memory of which conjures up the very essence of childhood. Yes, just about every one of us had his or her favorite Little Golden Book. Mine was *Mister Dog* by Margaret Wise Brown, illustrated by Garth Williams. It was about Crispin's Crispian, "The Dog Who Belonged to Himself," and I loved that little golden binding to shreds. Can you remember your favorite Little Golden Book? If so—and I'll bet you can—you'll want to join me in celebrating over sixty years of Little Golden Books.

It all began back in 1942, when World War II had most Americans clutching their purse strings. At a time when most children's books sold for about two dollars—making them luxury items for most families—a man named Georges Duplaix, president of a publishing company called Artists and Writers Guild, Inc., had a wonderful idea. What if you could manufacture a picture book that the average American family could afford? What if you sold that book in the place where that family went to shop every week for its food and sundries? What if you hired the very finest authors and illustrators to create the stories and pictures? That is how Little Golden Books were born, becoming surely one of the most important—and successful—experiments in publishing history.

Since their launch, more than two billion Little Golden Books have been printed—enough to reach all the way to the moon! By offering literary classics from esteemed authors and illustrators along with the pop-culture favorites of each decade (Howdy Doody, Roy Rogers, *Romper Room,* Bullwinkle, Scooby-Doo), Little Golden Books have found their way into the hands of millions of children through the simple strategy of creating high-quality stories at a price that's affordable for nearly everyone.

It's heartening to know that the demand for Little Golden Books remains as high today as it has ever been. Among the first Little Golden Books to be published, *The Poky Little Puppy* is the bestselling picture book of all time. This collection wouldn't be complete without it—or, for that matter, without the beloved *Home for a Bunny* and *The Saggy Baggy Elephant,* which, like *Poky,* have never been out of print.

The ten titles in this collection represent the work of many talented creators: authors Margaret Wise Brown, Ruth Krauss, Jane Werner Watson, Janette Sebring Lowrey, and Kathryn Jackson; and illustrators Tibor Gergely, Garth Williams, Gustaf Tenggren, Alice and Martin Provensen, and Mary Blair. These artists—all innovators— helped to shape and define the modern picture book.

How many happy hours have been enjoyed by generations poring over Little Golden Books? Isn't it reassuring that today—when it seems that everything is disposable—the timeless, often quirky, always friendly Little Golden Books are still here . . . ready to be read, reread, memorized, clamored for, chewed on, and loved to shreds by the youngest members of our marvelous world.

Kate Klimo
Publisher, Random House/Golden Books Young Readers Group
June 2003

The Poky Little Puppy

By Janette Sebring Lowrey
Illustrated by Gustaf Tenggren

The POKY LITTLE PUPPY

F IVE little puppies dug a hole under the fence
and went for a walk in the wide, wide world.
Through the meadow they went, down the
road, over the bridge, across the green grass, and
up the hill, one after the other.

And when they got to the top of the hill, they counted themselves: one, two, three, four. One little puppy wasn't there.

"Now where in the world is that poky little puppy?" they wondered. For he certainly wasn't on top of the hill.

He wasn't going down the other side.
The only thing they could see going down was
a fuzzy caterpillar.

He wasn't coming up this side. The only
thing they could see coming up was a quick
green lizard.

But when they looked down at the grassy place near the bottom of the hill, there he was, running round and round, his nose to the ground.

"What is he doing?" the four little puppies asked one another. And down they went to see, roly-poly, pell-mell, tumble-bumble, till they came to the green grass; and there they stopped short.

"What in the world are you doing?" they asked.

"I smell something!" said the poky little puppy.

Then the four little puppies began to sniff, and they smelled it, too.

"Rice pudding!" they said.

And home they went, as fast as they could go, over the bridge, up the road, through the meadow, and under the fence. And there, sure enough, was dinner waiting for them, with rice pudding for dessert.

But their mother was greatly displeased. "So you're the little puppies who dig holes under fences!" she said. "No rice pudding tonight!" And she made them go straight to bed.

But the poky little puppy came home after everyone was sound asleep.

He ate up the rice pudding and crawled into bed as happy as a lark.

The next morning someone had filled the hole and put up a sign. The sign said:

DON'T EVER DIG HOLES UNDER THIS FENCE!

BUT.....

The five little puppies dug a hole under the fence, just the same, and went for a walk in the wide, wide world.

Through the meadow they went, down the road, over the bridge, across the green grass, and up the hill, two and two. And when they got to the top of the hill, they counted themselves: one, two, three, four. One little puppy wasn't there.

"Now where in the world is that poky little puppy?" they wondered. For he certainly wasn't on top of the hill.

He wasn't going down the other side. The only thing they could see going down was a big black spider.

He wasn't coming up this side. The only thing they could see coming up was a brown hop-toad.

But when they looked down at the grassy place near the bottom of the hill, there was

the poky little puppy, sitting still as a stone, with his head on one side and his ears cocked up.

"What is he doing?" the four little puppies asked one another. And down they went to see, roly-poly, pell-mell, tumble-bumble, till they came to the green grass; and there they stopped short.

"What in the world are you doing?" they asked.

"I hear something!" said the poky little puppy.

The four little puppies listened, and they could hear it, too. "Chocolate custard!" they cried. "Someone is spooning it into our bowls!"

And home they went as fast as they could go, over the bridge, up the road, through the meadow, and under the fence. And there, sure enough, was dinner waiting for them, with chocolate custard for dessert.

But their mother was greatly displeased. "So you're the little puppies who will dig holes under fences!" she said. "No chocolate custard tonight!" And she made them go straight to bed.

But the poky little puppy came home after everyone else was sound asleep, and

he ate up all the chocolate custard and crawled into bed as happy as a lark.

The next morning someone had filled the hole and put up a sign.

The sign said:

BUT...

In spite of that, the five little puppies dug a hole under the fence and went for a walk in the wide, wide world.

Through the meadow they went, down the road, over the bridge, across the green grass, and up the hill, two and two. And when they got to the top of the hill, they counted themselves: one, two, three, four. One little puppy wasn't there.

"Now where in the world is that poky little puppy?" they wondered. For he certainly wasn't on top of the hill.

He wasn't going down the other side.
The only thing they could see going down was
a little grass snake.

He wasn't coming up this side. The only thing they could see coming up was a big grasshopper.

But when they looked down at the grassy place near the bottom of the hill, there he was, looking hard at something on the ground in front of him.

"What is he doing?" the four little puppies asked one another. And down they went to see, roly-poly, pell-mell, tumble-bumble, till they came to the green grass; and there they stopped short.

"What in the world are you doing?" they asked.

"I see something!" said the poky little puppy.

The four little puppies looked, and they could see it, too. It was a ripe, red strawberry growing there in the grass.

"Strawberry shortcake!" they cried.

And home they went as fast as they could go, over the bridge, up the road, through the meadow, and under the fence. And there, sure enough, was dinner waiting for them, with strawberry shortcake for dessert.

But their mother said: "So you're the little puppies who dug that hole under the fence again! No strawberry shortcake for supper tonight!" And she made them go straight to bed.

But the four little puppies waited till they thought she was asleep, and then they slipped out and filled up the hole, and when they turned around, there was their mother watching them.

"What good little puppies!" she said. "Come have some strawberry shortcake!"

And this time, when the poky little puppy got home, he had to squeeze in through a wide place in the fence. And there were his four brothers and sisters, licking the last crumbs from their saucer.

"Dear me!" said his mother. "What a pity you're so poky! Now the strawberry shortcake is all gone!"

So the poky little puppy had to go to bed without a single bite of shortcake, and he felt very sorry for himself.

And the next morning someone had put up a sign that read:

NO DESSERTS EVER UNLESS PUPPIES NEVER DIG HOLES UNDER THIS FENCE AGAIN!

Scuffy the Tugboat

By Gertrude Crampton

Illustrated by Tibor Gergely

Scuffy was sad.
Scuffy was cross.
Scuffy sniffed his blue smokestack.

"A toy store is no place for a red-painted tugboat," said Scuffy, and he sniffed his blue smokestack again. "I was meant for bigger things."

"Perhaps you would not be cross if you went sailing," said the man with the polka dot tie, who owned the shop.

So one night he took Scuffy home to his little boy. He filled the bathtub with water.

"Sail, little tugboat," said the little boy.

"I won't sail in a bathtub," said Scuffy. "A tub is no place for a red-painted tugboat. I was meant for bigger things."

The next day the man with the polka dot tie and his little boy carried Scuffy to a laughing brook that started high in the hills.

"Sail, little tugboat," said the man with the polka dot tie.

It was Spring, and the brook was full to the
brim with its water. And the water moved in a
hurry, as all things move in a hurry when it is
Spring.

Scuffy was in a hurry, too.

"Come back, little tugboat, come back," cried the little boy as the hurrying, brimful brook carried Scuffy downstream.

"Not I," tooted Scuffy. "Not I. This is the life for me."

All that day Scuffy sailed along with the brook.
Past the meadows filled with cowslips. Past the
women washing clothes on the bank. Past the
little woods filled with violets.

Cows came to the brook to drink.

They stood in the cool water, and it was fun

to sail around between their legs and bump softly into their noses.

It was fun to see them drink.

But when a white and brown cow almost drank Scuffy instead of the brook's cool water, Scuffy was frightened. That was not fun!

Night came, and with it the moon.

There was nothing to see but the quiet trees.

Suddenly an owl called out, "Hoot! Hooot!"

"Toot, tooot!" cried the frightened tugboat, and he wished he could see the smiling face of the man with the polka dot tie.

When morning came, Scuffy was cross instead of frightened.

"I was meant for bigger things, but which way am I to go?" he said. But there was only one way to go, and that was with the running water where the two brooks met to form a small river. And with the river sailed Scuffy, the red-painted tugboat.

He was proud when he sailed past villages.

"People build villages at the edge of my river," said Scuffy, and he straightened his blue smokestack.

Once Scuffy's river joined a small one jammed with logs. Here were men in heavy jackets and great boots, walking about on the floating logs, trying to pry them free.

"Toot, toot, let me through," demanded Scuffy. But the men paid no attention to him. They pushed the logs apart so they would drift with the river to the sawmill in the town. Scuffy bumped along with the jostling logs.

"Ouch!" he cried as two logs bumped together.

"This is a fine river," said Scuffy, "but it's very busy and very big for me."

He was proud when he sailed under the bridges.

"My river is so wide and so deep that people must build bridges to cross it."

The river moved through big towns now instead of villages.

And the bridges over it were very wide—wide enough so that many cars and trucks and streetcars could cross all at once.

The river got deeper and deeper. Scuffy did not have to tuck up his bottom.

The river moved faster and faster.

"I feel like a train instead of a tugboat," said Scuffy, as he was hurried along.

He was proud when he passed the old saw mill with its water wheel.

But high in the hills and mountains the winter snow melted. Water filled the brooks and rushed from there into the small rivers. Faster and faster it flowed, to the great river where Scuffy sailed.

"There is too much water in this river," said Scuffy, as he pitched and tossed on the waves. "Soon it will splash over the top and what a flood there will be!"

Soon great armies of men came to save the fields and towns from the rushing water.

They filled bags with sand and put them at the edge of the river.

"They're making higher banks for the river," shouted Scuffy, "to hold the water back." The water rose higher and higher.

The men built the sand bags higher and higher. Higher! went the river. Higher! went the sand bags.

At last the water rose no more. The flood water rushed on to the sea, and Scuffy raced along with the flood. The people and the fields and the towns were safe.

On went the river to the sea. At last Scuffy sailed into a big city. Here the river widened, and all about were docks and wharves.

Oh, it was a busy place and a noisy place! The cranes groaned as they swung the cargoes into great ships. The porters shouted as they carried suitcases and boxes on board.

Horses stamped and truck motors roared, streetcars clanged and people shouted. Scuffy said, "Toot, toot," but nobody noticed.

"Oh, oh!" cried Scuffy when he saw the sea. "There is no beginning and there is no end to the sea. I wish I could find the man with the polka dot tie and his little boy!"

Just as the little red-painted tugboat sailed past the last piece of land, a hand reached out and picked him up. And there was the man with the polka dot tie, with his little boy beside him.

Scuffy is home now with the man with the polka dot tie and his little boy.

He sails from one end of the bathtub to the other.

"This is the place for a red-painted tugboat," said Scuffy. "And this is the life for me."

The Saggy Baggy Elephant

By Kathryn and Byron Jackson
Illustrated by Gustaf Tenggren

THE SAGGY BAGGY
ELEPHANT

A happy little elephant was dancing through the jungle. He thought he was dancing beautifully, one-two-three-kick. But whenever he went one-two-three, his big feet pounded so that they shook the whole jungle. And whenever he went kick, he kicked over a tree or a bush.

The little elephant danced along leaving wreckage behind him, until one day, he met a parrot.

"Why are you shaking the jungle all to pieces?" cried the parrot, who had never before seen an elephant. "What kind of animal are you, anyway?"

The little elephant said, "I don't know what kind of animal I am. I live all alone in the jungle. I dance and I kick—and I call myself Sooki. It's a good-sounding name, and it fits me, don't you think?"

"Maybe," answered the parrot, "but if it does it's the only thing that *does* fit you. Your ears are too big for you, and your nose is way too big for you. And your skin is *much,* MUCH too big for you. It's baggy and saggy. You should call yourself Saggy-Baggy!"

Sooki sighed. His pants *did* look pretty wrinkled.

"I'd be glad to improve myself," he said, "but I don't know how to go about it. What shall I do?"

"I can't tell you. I never saw anything like you in all my life!" replied the parrot.

The little elephant tried to smooth out his skin.
He rubbed it with his trunk. That did no good.

He pulled up his pants legs—but they fell right back into dozens of wrinkles.

It was very disappointing, and the parrot's saucy laugh didn't help a bit.

Just then a tiger came walking along. He was a beautiful, sleek tiger. His skin fit him like a glove.

Sooki rushed up to him and said:

"Tiger, please tell me why your skin fits so well! The parrot says mine is all baggy and saggy,

and I do want to make it fit me like yours fits you!"

The tiger didn't care a fig about Sooki's troubles, but he did feel flattered and important, and he did feel just a little mite hungry.

"My skin always did fit," said the tiger. "Maybe it's because I take a lot of exercise. But . . ." added the tiger, ". . . if you don't care for exercise, I shall be delighted to nibble a few of those extra pounds of skin off for you!"

"Oh no, thank you! No, thank you!" cried Sooki. "I love exercise! Just watch me!"

Sooki ran until he was well beyond reach.

Then he did somersaults and rolled on his back. He walked on his hind legs and he walked on his front legs.

When Sooki wandered down to the river to get a big drink of water, he met the parrot. The parrot laughed harder than ever.

"I tried exercising," sighed the little elephant. "Now I don't know what to do."

"Soak in the water the way the crocodile does," laughed the parrot. "Maybe your skin will shrink."

So Sooki tramped straight into the water.

But before he had soaked nearly long enough to shrink his skin, a great big crocodile came swimming up, snapping his fierce jaws and looking greedily at Sooki's tender ears.

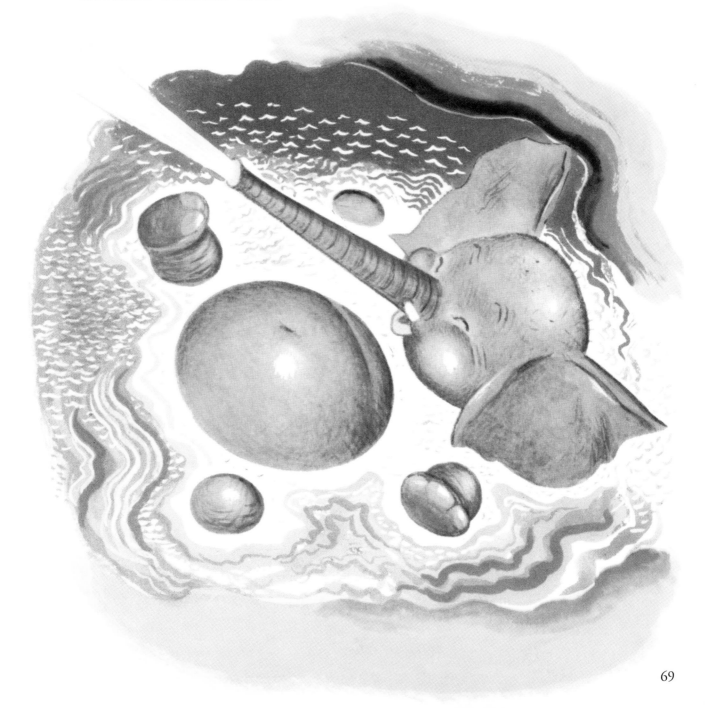

The little elephant clambered up the bank and ran away, feeling very discouraged.

"I'd better hide in a dark place where my bags and sags and creases and wrinkles won't show," he said.

By and by he found a deep dark cave, and with a heavy sigh he tramped inside and sat down.

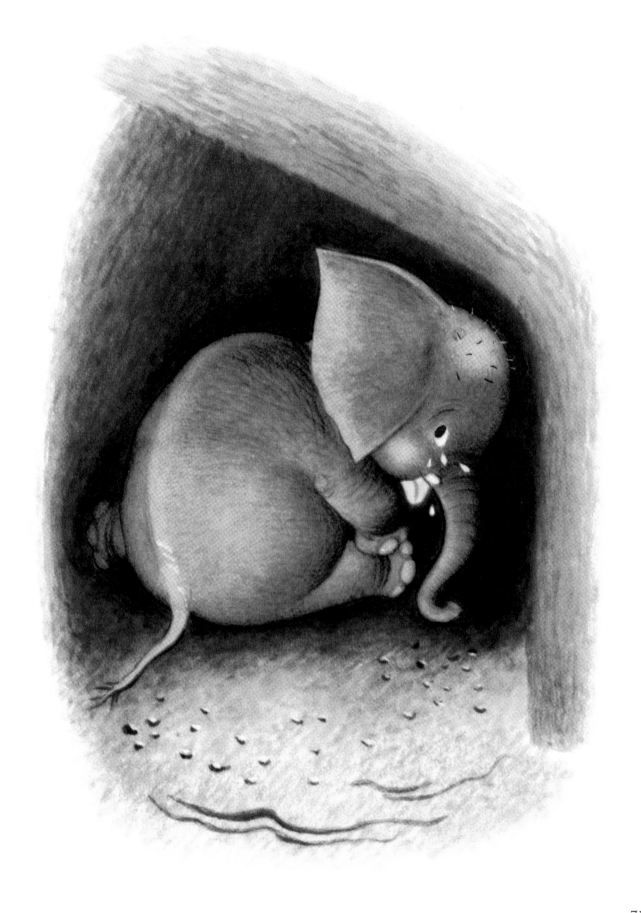

Suddenly, he heard a fierce growling and grumbling and snarling. He peeped out of the cave and saw a lion padding down the path.

"I'm hungry!" roared the lion. "I haven't had a thing to eat today. Not a thing except a thin, bony antelope, and a puny monkey—and a buffalo, but such a tough one! And two turtles, but you can't count turtles. There's nothing much to eat between those saucers they wear for clothes! I'm *hungry!* I could eat an *elephant!*"

And he began to pad straight toward the dark cave where the little elephant was hidden.

"This is the end of me, sags, bags, wrinkles and all," thought Sooki, and he let out one last, trumpeting bellow!

Just as he did, the jungle was filled with a terrible crashing and an awful stomping. A whole herd of great gray wrinkled elephants came charging up, and the big hungry lion jumped up in the air, turned around, and ran away as fast as he could go.

Sooki peeped out of the cave and all the big elephants smiled at him. Sooki thought they were the most beautiful creatures he had ever seen.

"I wish I looked just like you," he said.

"You do," grinned the big elephants. "You're a perfectly dandy little elephant!"

And that made Sooki so happy that he began to

dance one-two-three-kick through the jungle, with all those big, brave, friendly elephants behind him. The saucy parrot watched them dance. But this time he didn't laugh, not even to himself.

The Fuzzy Duckling

By Jane Werner Watson

Illustrated by Alice and Martin Provensen

The Fuzzy
Duckling

Early one bright morning
a small fuzzy duckling went for a walk.
He walked through the sunshine.
He walked through the shade.

In the long striped shadows
that the cattails made
he met two frisky colts.

"Hello," said the duckling.
"Will you come for a walk with me?"

But the two frisky colts would not.

So on went the little duckling,
on over the hill.

There he found three spotted calves,
all resting in the shade.
"Hello," said the duckling.
"Will you come for a walk with me?"

But the sleepy calves would not.
So on went the duckling.

He met four noisy turkeys

and five white geese

and six lively lambs
with thick soft fleece.

But no one would come for a walk
with the fuzzy duckling.
So on he went, all by his lone.

He met seven playful puppies

and eight hungry pigs.
"Won't you come for a walk with me?"
asked the fuzzy duckling.

"You had better walk straight home,"
said the pigs.
"Don't you know it's suppertime?"

"Oh," said the duckling. "Thank you."
But which way was home?

Just as he began to feel quite unhappy,
he heard a sound in the rushes nearby . . .
and out waddled nine fuzzy ducklings
with their big mother duck.

"At last," said the mother duck.
"Here is our lost baby duckling."

"Get in line," called the other ducklings.
"We're going home for supper."

So the lost little duckling joined the line,
and away went the ten little ducklings,
home for supper.

"This is the best way to go for a walk,"
said the happy little, fuzzy little duck.

I Can Fly

By Ruth Krauss
Illustrated by Mary Blair

A bird can fly.
So can I.

A cow can moo.

I can too.

I can squirm

like a worm.

I can grab

like a crab.

Crunch crunch crunch

I'm a goat out to lunch.

Who's busy like a bee?

Me me me.

Who can walk like a bug?

Me! Ug ug.

I'm merrier

than a terrier.

Swish!

I'm a fish.

Pick pick pick

I'm a little chick.

Who can live in a hole?

Me! Like a mole.

Who can climb anywhere?

Me! Like a bear.

My house is

like a mouse's.

A clam

is what I am.

Pop pop pop

I'm a rabbit with a hop.

Bump bump bump

I'm a camel with a hump.

Haw haw haw

I'm a donkey in the straw.

Pitter pitter pat

I can walk like a cat.

Howl howl howl

I'm an old screech owl.

146

Gubble gubble gubble
I'm a mubble in a pubble.
I can play
I'm anything that's anything.
That's MY way.

I CAN FLY

Gayly   Words by Hilda Marx   Music by Alec Wilder

mf   I can fly like a bird, I can

swim like a fish, I can grab like a crab, I can be what I wish.

Just by pre - tend - ing all through the day, I can be an - y - thing

I want to play — That's my way.

Seven Little Postmen

By Margaret Wise Brown and Edith Thacher Hurd
Illustrated by Tibor Gergely

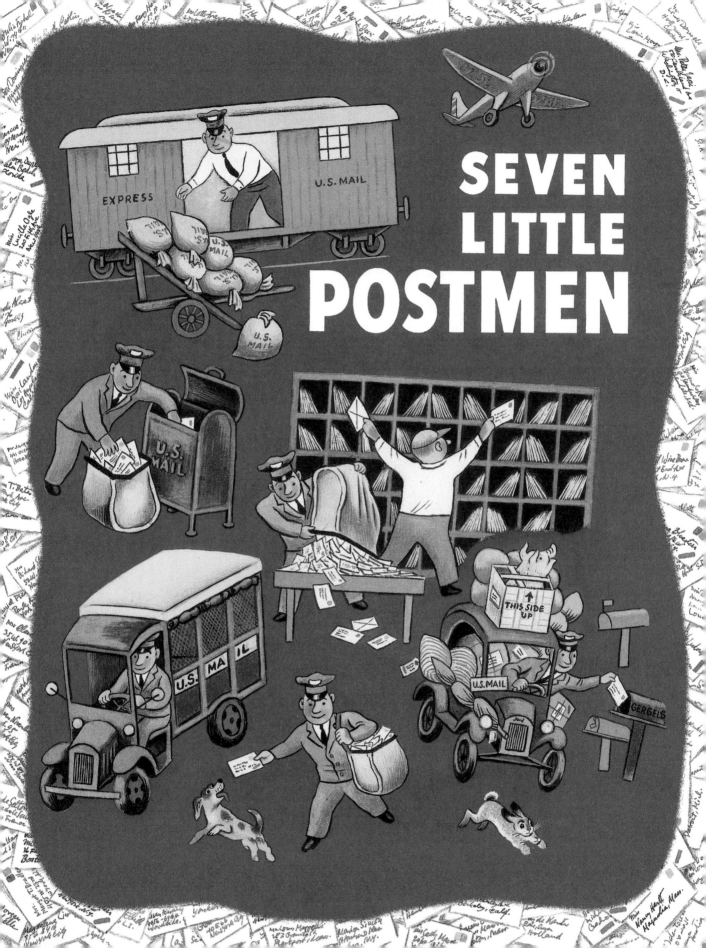

A boy had a secret. It was a surprise.
He wanted to tell his grandmother.
So he sent his secret through the mail.
The story of that letter
Is the reason for this tale
Of the seven little postmen who carried the mail.

Because there was a secret in the letter
The boy sealed it with red sealing wax.
If anyone broke the seal
The secret would be out.

He slipped the letter into the mail box.

The first little postman
Took it from the box,
Put it in his bag,
And walked seventeen blocks
To a big Post Office
All built of rocks.

The letter with the secret
Was dumped on a table
With big and small letters
That all needed the label
Of the big Post Office.

Stamp stamp, clickety click,
The machinery ran with a quick sharp tick.
The letter with the secret is stamped at last
And the round black circle tells that it passed
Through the cancelling machine
      Click   whizz   fast!

Big letters
Small letters
Thin and tall—
The second little postman
Sorts them all.
The letters are sorted
From East to West
From North to South.

"And this letter
Had best go West,"
Said the second
Little postman,
Scratching his chest.
Into the pouch
Lock it tight
The secret letter
Must travel all night.

The third little postman in the big mail car
Comes to a crossroad where waiting are
A green, a yellow, and a purple car.
They all stop there. There is nothing to say.
The mail truck has the right of way!
"The mail must go through!"

Up and away through sleet and hail
This airplane carries the fastest mail.
The pilot flies through whirling snow
As far and as fast as the plane can go.

The mail is landed for the evening train.
Now hang the pouch on the big hook crane!
The engine speeds up the shining rails
And the fourth little postman
Grabs the mail with a giant hook.

The train roars on
With a puff and a snort
And the fourth little postman
Begins to sort.

The train carries the letter
Through gloom of night
In a mail car filled with electric light

To a country postman
By a country road
Where the fifth little postman
Is waiting for his load.

The mail clerk
Heaves the mail pouch
With all his might
To the fifth little postman
Who grabs it tight.

Then off he goes
Along the lane
And over the hill
Until
He comes to a little town
That is very small—
So very small
The Post Office there
Is hardly one at all.

The sixth little postman
In great big boots
Sorts the letters
For their various routes—
Some down the river,
Some over the hill.

But the secret letter
Goes farther still.

The seventh little postman on R.F.D.
Carries letters and papers, chickens and fruit
To the people who live along his route.

There were parts
For a tractor

And a wig for an actor

And a funny post card
For a little boy
Playing in his own backyard.

There was something for Sally
And something for Sam

And something for Mrs. Potter
Who was busy making jam.

There were dozens of chickens
For Mrs. Pickens

And a dress for a party
For Mrs. McCarty.

At the last house along the way sat the grandmother of the boy who had sent the letter with the secret in it. She had been wishing all day he would come to visit. For she lived all alone in a tiny house and sometimes felt quite lonely.

The postman blew his whistle and gave her the letter with the red sealing wax on it— the secret letter!

"Sakes alive! What is it about?"
Sakes alive! The secret is out!
What does it say?

DEAREST GRANNY:
I AM WRITING TO SAY

THAT I'M COMING TO VISIT ON SATURDAY.
MY CAT HAS SEVEN KITTENS AND I AM BRINGING
ONE TO YOU FOR YOUR VERY OWN KITTEN.
THE POSTMAN IS #5 MY FRIEND.
                    YOUR GRANDSON
                        THOMAS

SEVEN LITTLE POSTMEN

Seven Little Postmen carried the mail
Through Rain and Snow and Wind and Hail
Through Snow and Rain and Gloom of Night

Seven Little Postmen
Out of sight.
Over Land and Sea
Through Air and Light
Through Snow and Rain
And Gloom of Night—
Put a stamp on your letter
And seal it tight.

Home for a Bunny

By Margaret Wise Brown
Illustrated by Garth Williams

HOME FOR A BUNNY

"Spring, Spring, Spring!"
sang the frog.
"Spring!" said the groundhog.

"Spring, Spring, Spring!"
sang the robin.
It was Spring.
The leaves burst out.
The flowers burst out.
And robins burst out of their eggs.
It was Spring.

In the Spring a bunny
came down the road.
He was going to find
a home of his own.
A home for a bunny,
A home of his own,
Under a rock,
Under a stone,
Under a log,
Or under the ground.
Where would a bunny find a home?

"Where is your home?"
he asked the robin.

"Here, here, here,"
sang the robin.
"Here in this nest is my home."

"Here, here, here,"
sang the little robins who were
about to fall out of the nest.
"Here is our home."

"Not for me," said the bunny.
"I would fall out of a nest.
I would fall on the ground."

So he went on
looking for a home.
"Where is your home?"
he asked a frog.

"Wog, wog, wog,"
sang the frog.
"Wog, wog, wog,
Under the water,
Down in the bog."
"Not for me,"
said the bunny.
"Under the water,
I would drown in a bog."

So he went on
looking for a home.
"Where do you live?"
he asked the groundhog.
"In a log," said the groundhog.
"Can I come in?" said the bunny.
"No, you can't come in my log,"
said the groundhog.

So the bunny went down the road.
  Down the road
and down the road he went.
  He was going to find
a home of his own.
  A home for a bunny,
  A home of his own,
  Under a rock
  Or a log
  Or a stone.
  Where would a bunny find a home?

Down the road
and down the road
and down the road
he went, until—

He met a bunny.
"Where is your home?"
he asked the bunny.

"Here," said the bunny.
"Here is my home.
Under this rock,
Under this stone,
Down under the ground,
Here is my home."

"Can I come in?"
said the bunny.
"Yes," said the bunny.
And so he did.

Animal Orchestra

By Ilo Orleans
Illustrated by Tibor Gergely

Animal Orchestra

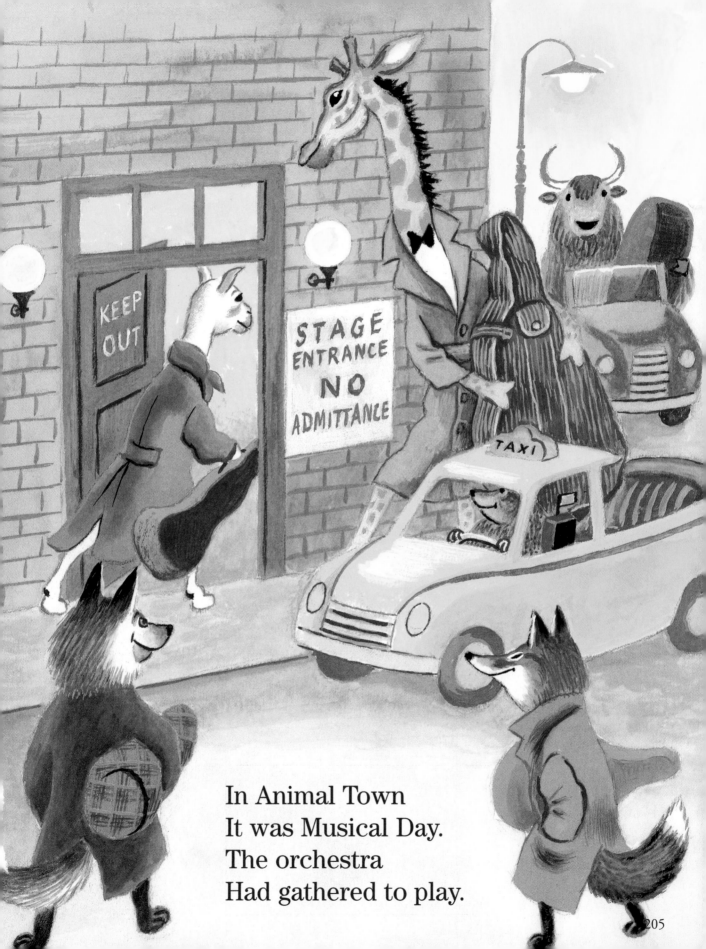

In Animal Town
It was Musical Day.
The orchestra
Had gathered to play.

Everyone came
To hear and to see.

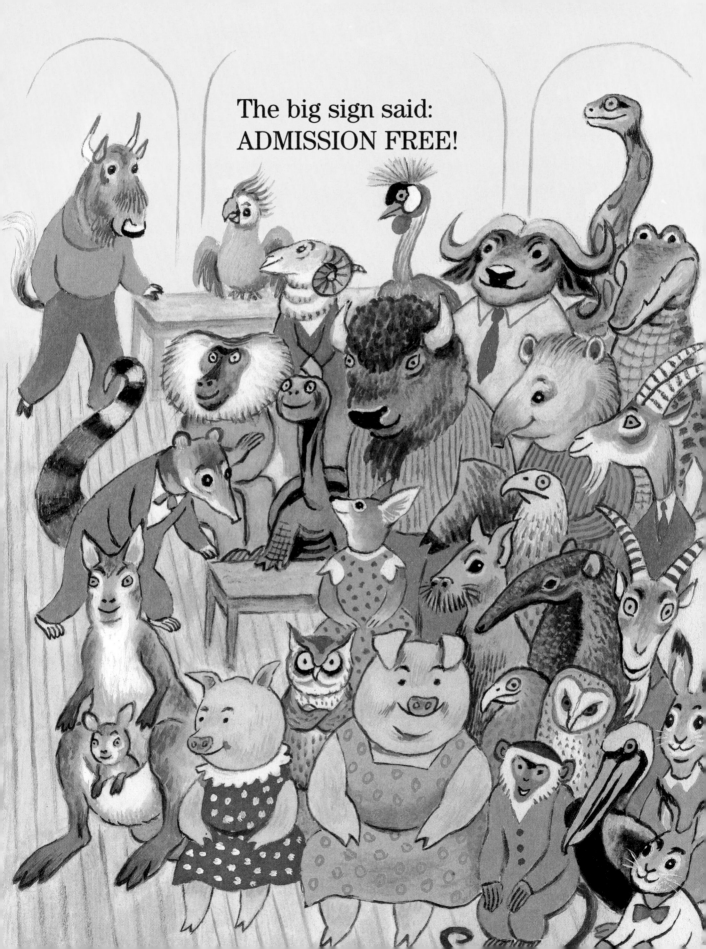

The big sign said:
ADMISSION FREE!

Up to the platform
Each animal went,

And proudly carried
His instrument.

Then came the conductor
With stick in his hand—
The handsomest Hippo
In Animal Land.
He tapped his foot.
He waved his hand,
And cried to the players:
"Strike up the band!"

The gray Seals barked.
They lifted their fins,
And tweedled upon
Their violins.

The spotted Giraffes—
The oddest fellows—
Zoomed and zoomed
On their yellow cellos.

The Lion bugled;
The Rhino fluted;

The Leopard harped;
The Tiger tooted.

The Monkey wiggled
A brass trombone.
The Llama blew
A saxophone.

The Elephant
Kept trumpeting.
The Camel plucked
His mandolin string.

Upon his cymbals
The Bear clang-clanged.

Upon his guitar
The Fox twang-twanged!

The Yak beat the drum;
The Wolf played the fife.
Each beast was enjoying
The time of his life.

219

They whistled! They fiddled!
They thumped! They blew!

What a roar! What a din!
What a great to-do!

The animal girls—
The animal boys—
The animal audience
Made a great noise.

222

They slapped their tails,
They clapped their paws,
And that is how
They made applause!

The conductor bowed,
And bowed and bowed.

All of the orchestra
Players were proud.

The Hippo was happy
On Musical Day,
For everyone shouted:
"Hip-HIPPO-ray!"

The Lion's Paw

By Jane Werner Watson

Illustrated by Gustaf Tenggren

The Lion's Paw

"Ow!" roared the lion.
"There is a thorn in my paw.
Who will take it out?"

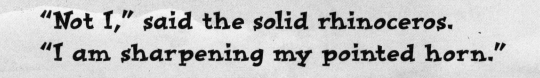

"Not I," said the solid rhinoceros.
"I am sharpening my pointed horn."

"Not I," said the startled kudu.
"I am racing away from here!"

"Not I," whispered the tall
giraffe among the tip-top leaves.

"Not I," said the bouncing baboon.
"I am having too much fun."

"Who will take the thorn out?"
asked the crowned crane.

"Not I," said the hippopotamus.
"I am cooling off in the mud."

237

"Not I," said the striped zebra.
"I am kicking up my heels."

"Not I," said the bright-eyed monkey.
"I am swinging by my tail."

"Not I," said the big gorilla.
"I am scratching away my fleas."

"Not I," said the elegant gazelle.
"I am leaping across the veld."

"Will no one remove the thorn?"
called the ibis by the purple pool.

"Not I," said the slippery crocodile,
smiling a hungry smile.

"Not I," said the trumpeting elephant.
"I am taking a shower."

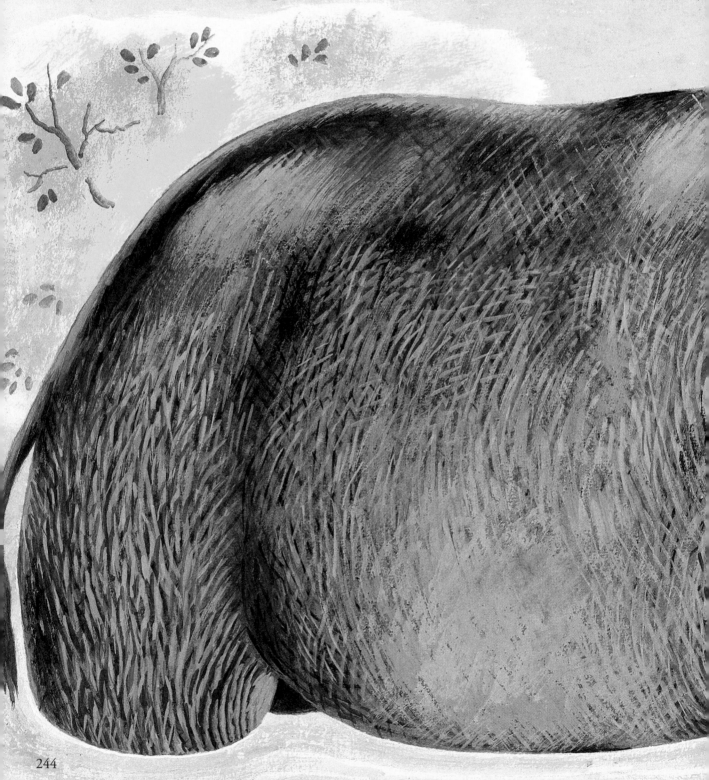

"Not I," said the spotted leopard.
"I am slinking through the shade."

"Not I," said the solemn buffalo.
"I have too much work to do."

"Who will help the lion?" cried the
ostrich running over the desert sands.

"Not I," said the sulky camel.
"I am chewing my chewy cud."

249

"Not I," said the swooping vulture.
"I'm busy hunting a meal."

"Not I," said the fast cheetah.
"I'm busy hunting, too."

"I will," said the little mouse.
And she did!

The Good Humor® Man

By Kathleen N. Daly

Illustrated by Tibor Gergely

Ting-a-ling-a-ling!

"Here comes the Good Humor man," yelled
Danny.

He slid down from the tree and grabbed his
little sister's hand and off they ran to see the
Good Humor man.

Tommy left his trains

and Dinah left her dolls

and Katie left her kittens

and Bobby left his boats

and they ran down the street
to see the Good Humor man.

Mothers left their kitchens
and daddies left their lawn mowers
and dogs left their bones.

Everybody was there to see the friendly
Good Humor man in his little white truck.

"What flavor would you like?"
asked the Good Humor man.
"There are walnut whizzes,
And dairy dizzies,
Chocolate chips
And strawberry splits."

"There are lemonade licks
And syrupy sticks,
Raspberry rockets
And pineapple pockets.
And my special flavor for today
Is Fun Valley Smash:
Raspberry-strawberry-marshmallow mash."
Oh, my they did taste good.

The Good Humor man was *just* about to leave when along came little Johnny Slow-Poke with his fat puppy.

The Good Humor man gave him a pineapple pinnacle, and off he went, *ting-a-ling-a-ling*.

264

He stopped at George's Garage, so that all the
hungry drivers on the highway could see him.

He stopped at Piney Crest Pond, and the hot little sailors (and their daddies) stopped to greet him.

He stopped at Cherry Tree Corner, and the busy
road workers stopped for a cool ice cream.

Then he made a special stop at the cottage up
on the hill. There lived old Granny Griggs and her
small grandson Dick, who had just come to stay.

"I want an extra-special treat for Dick," said
Granny Griggs. "I don't know any children, and I'm
afraid he finds it a bit lonely up here."

The Good Humor man gave Dick a friendly flakey
frostee and went on his way, *ting-a-ling-a-ling*.

"It's been a long, hot day," thought the Good Humor man, as he drove through the peppermint gates of Fun Valley.

It is there, you know, that ice creams are made,
and it's there that all the little white trucks live.

The next day, *ting-a-ling-a-ling*, the Good
Humor man made his rounds again. Along came
Danny and Tommy and Dinah and Katie and Bobby
and all the mothers and daddies.

The Good Humor man was *just* about to leave—
but where was Johnny Slow-Poke? *There* he was,
and he was crying.

"I've lost my puppy!" wailed Johnny.

The Good Humor man shook his head sadly and
handed Johnny a comforting coconut cone.

He stopped at George's Garage

and Piney Crest Pond

and Cherry Tree Corner.

273

Then he went to the cottage on the hill,
ting-a-ling-a-ling.

"Look, look, I've found a puppy!" yelled Dick.

"Why, Dick, that's Johnny Slow-Poke's puppy,"
said the Good Humor man. "He *will* be glad
it's found!"

The Good Humor man told them where Johnny
lived, and Dick and Granny Griggs set out to find him.
And the Good Humor man went on his way,
ting-a-ling-a-ling, back to Fun Valley.

The next day, when all the children and mothers
and daddies had gotten their ice cream and the
Good Humor man was *just* about to drive away,
who should come along but little Johnny Slow-
Poke and his fat puppy.

And right beside them was little Dick Griggs!
"Look, I've found my puppy!" said Johnny.
"And look, I've found a friend!" said Dick.

"Oh my," said the Good Humor man. "Today you'll
need something *very* good:
"There are peppermint pearls and wonderful whirls,
Tangerine treats and nutty nougat neats.
And my *special* flavor today is Fun Valley Flip:
Butterscotch-apricot-coconut chip."

And as the Good Humor man drove off that afternoon he gave an extra-specially happy *ting-a-ling-a-ling* on his bell.

Biographies
and
A Brief History of
Little Golden Books

Biographies

MARY BLAIR (1911–1978) illustrated several Golden Books, including *The Up and Down Book, Baby's House,* and *The Golden Book of Little Verses.* For nearly four decades, she was involved with many important Disney projects. She created the concept sketches for such animated feature films as *Cinderella, Alice in Wonderland,* and *Peter Pan,* and designed the 1964–65 New York World's Fair exhibit "It's a Small World." To recognize her creative contributions, the Disney Company named Mary Blair a Disney Legend in 1991.

MARGARET WISE BROWN (1910–1952) wrote some of the most popular children's books of all time, including *Goodnight Moon* and *The Runaway Bunny.* She was keenly aware that children were captivated by the sights and sounds of the everyday world, and she understood their need for love, security, and a place to belong. She wrote many classic Golden Books, such as *The Golden Egg Book, Home for a Bunny, The Sailor Dog, The Color Kittens, Mister Dog,* and *The Friendly Book.*

GERTRUDE CRAMPTON is the author of two of the bestselling children's books of all time: *Tootle* and *Scuffy the Tugboat,* both Little Golden Books. They have been translated into many languages and have never been out of print.

KATHLEEN N. DALY (b. 1930) was born in London. She grew up in France and Scotland and on the island of Mauritius. She worked as a children's book editor for Blackie & Son in London in the early 1950s and became the editor of Little Golden Books in New York in 1953. She wrote many Golden Books while on staff and for years afterward. A versatile writer, she created nonfiction titles *(My Elephant Book)* as well as more fanciful tales *(The Four Little Kittens).* She now resides once again in London.

TIBOR GERGELY (1900–1978) illustrated more than seventy Golden Books. Born in Budapest, Hungary, he received his only formal art schooling in Vienna, at age twenty, and began to work as a designer of stage sets and marionettes. For several years he also worked as a caricaturist for Viennese newspapers. During that time he painted murals and exhibited his paintings in Europe. In 1939, Gergely rolled up his canvases and immigrated to the United States, settling in New York. His long association with Little Golden Books began in 1942—the year of their launch—and continued as long as he lived. Gergely brought to life two of the most famous Little Golden Books, *Tootle* and *Scuffy the Tugboat.* Other best-loved Golden Books illustrated by Gergely are *The Great Big Fire Engine Book* and *The Taxi That Hurried.* In 1955, *Wheel on the Chimney,* written by Margaret Wise Brown, illustrated by Gergely, and published by Lippincott, was named a Caldecott Honor Book.

KATHRYN and BYRON JACKSON cowrote hundreds of stories for Golden Books, many of them for large collections such as *Pirates, Ships, and Sailors* and *Tenggren's Farm Stories. The Saggy Baggy Elephant* is one of their most famous books. Kathryn

Jackson also wrote such Golden Books classics as *Tawny Scrawny Lion, Pantaloon,* and *Richard Scarry's A Story a Day: 365 Stories and Rhymes.*

RUTH KRAUSS (1901–1993) was a poet, a playwright, and a groundbreaking author of children's books. She was a keen observer of children and one of the first authors to capture their language and perspective. "I thought of my books as a way of returning the material to the kids," she once said. Krauss enjoyed collaborating with such ingenious illustrators as Maurice Sendak, Marc Simont, and her husband, Crockett Johnson. Two of her best-known titles are *A Hole Is to Dig: A First Book of First Definitions* and *The Carrot Seed,* which she listed among her favorites.

JANETTE SEBRING LOWREY (1892–1986) has the distinction of being the author of *The Poky Little Puppy,* the bestselling picture book of all time. She wrote several other Little Golden Books, as well as young adult novels for other publishers. A native Texan, Janette Sebring Lowrey received the 1964 Texas Institute of Letters Award for the best young adult book of the year, *Love, Bid Me Welcome* (Harper).

ILO ORLEANS (1897–1962) was a London-born lawyer who attained national prominence as a writer of poetry for children. A year after he graduated from Columbia University in 1916, he enrolled in Columbia Law School, where he was editor of the *Columbia Law Review* until he earned his diploma in 1919. He wrote more than ten children's books, including *Funday, Wonder Book of Fun,* and *I Watch the World Go By.* His numerous poems appeared in *Jack and Jill* and *Highlights for Children,* as well as textbooks, anthologies, music books, and teachers' manuals throughout the English-speaking world. More than twenty of his devotional poems were set to music for use by school and church groups of all faiths. In 1956, Orleans received the Hayil Honor Award for his contribution to devotional writing for children.

ALICE (b. 1918) and MARTIN (1916–1987) PROVENSEN began to illustrate children's books together in 1946, many of them for Golden Books. Besides *The Fuzzy Duckling,* the Provensens illustrated *The Animal Fair, The Golden Mother Goose, The Iliad and the Odyssey,* and *The Color Kittens,* one of the most beloved Little Golden Books of all time. The couple was awarded the Caldecott Medal in 1984 for *The Glorious Flight: Across the Channel with Louis Blériot* (Viking). *A Visit to William Blake's Inn: Poems for Innocent and Experienced Travelers* (Harcourt) was a 1982 Caldecott Honor Book.

GUSTAF TENGGREN (1896–1970) was a beloved illustrator in his native Sweden and in Denmark long before he came to the United States in 1920. His books have been published in almost every country of the world. Besides illustrating children's books, he provided the concept art for the Walt Disney films *Snow White and the Seven Dwarfs* and *Pinocchio.* Gustaf Tenggren was the illustrator of many classic Golden Books, including *The Saggy Baggy Elephant, The Big Brown Bear,* and *The Poky Little Puppy*—one of the most popular children's books of all time—as well as treasuries such as *Tenggren's Golden Tales from the Arabian Nights* and *King Arthur and the Knights of the Round Table.*

Tenggren was posthumously awarded a Kerlan Award in 2003.

JANE WERNER WATSON (b. 1915) was an editor and prolific author of Golden Books. She wrote more than 150 Golden titles, featuring a wide variety of subjects and characters. During her long career, which spanned the years from 1938 to 1954, she edited dozens of favorite Golden Books, including *The Giant Golden Old and New Testaments, The Giant Golden History of the World,* and *Giant Golden Dinosaurs.* In 1958, the *Los Angeles Times* named her Woman of the Year for Literature. Jane Werner Watson traveled extensively and lived in India for several years. In 1964, she received an award from the government of India for the contributions she made to literacy there with her book *Aab Hom Azad Hung* (*Now We Are Free;* Rajkamal

Prakashan Printers Ltd., Delhi), one of ten books for beginning readers on East Indian subjects.

GARTH WILLIAMS (1912–1996) is known for his realistic yet highly expressive animal characters. For decades, children have been unable to resist patting the "fur" of his appealing creatures. His unique style has brought to life some of the best-loved children's books of the twentieth century, including E. B. White's *Stuart Little* and *Charlotte's Web* and the Little House series by Laura Ingalls Wilder. He illustrated many timeless Golden Books, among them *Home for a Bunny, The Sailor Dog, The Kitten Who Thought He Was a Mouse, Mister Dog,* and *The Friendly Book.*

A Brief History of Little Golden Books

Before 1942, children's books normally sold for about two dollars, a luxury for many families. Georges Duplaix, president of Artists and Writers Guild, Inc. (a joint interest of Simon & Schuster Publishing and Western Printing), came up with the concept of developing a colorful children's book that was durable and affordable for most American families.

> **LITTLE GOLDEN BOOKS**
> ❀ **1940s** ❀
> **AVERAGE COST: 25¢**

September 1942: Simon & Schuster publishes the very first Little Golden Book. The original twelve titles included the following:

The Poky Little Puppy

Three Little Kittens

Bedtime Stories

The Alphabet A–Z

Mother Goose

Prayers for Children

The Little Red Hen

Nursery Songs

The Golden Book of Fairy Tales

Baby's Book

The Animals of Farmer Jones

This Little Piggy

September 19, 1942: The first advertisement announcing Little Golden Books appears in *Publishers Weekly.*

February 1943: After five short months, the original twelve Little Golden Books are in their third printing, with a total of 1.5 million copies in print.

1944: Simon & Schuster launches a separate Little Golden Books division called Sandpiper Press, headed by Georges Duplaix.

1944: The first Walt Disney Little Golden Book, *Through the Picture Frame,* is published.

1945: Most of the original twelve Little Golden Books are now in their seventh printing.

> **LITTLE GOLDEN BOOKS**
> ❀ **1950s–1970s** ❀
> **AVERAGE COST:**
> **25¢ (1952) 29¢ (1962)**
> **39¢ (1968) 59¢ (1977)**

1951: *Doctor Dan, The Bandage Man* is published with six Johnson & Johnson Band-Aids® glued to the right side of the title page. The first printing is 1.75 million—the largest first printing of any Little Golden Book to date.

1952: Little Golden Books' tenth anniversary. Nearly 183 million Little Golden Books have been sold, with *The Night Before Christmas* alone selling more than 4 million copies.

1953: In just over ten years, almost 300 million Little Golden Books have been sold.

More than half of the titles printed by 1954 have sold over a million copies each.

1954: Little Golden Books are now available throughout most of the world, except in the Soviet Union.

May 1, 1954: Release of *Little Lulu and Her Magic Tricks,* with a 2.25 million first printing. The book has a small package of Kleenex® tissues attached to its front cover and directions for making toys from the tissues. An extensive advertising and promotional campaign for this title leads to the book's appearance on the *Arthur Godfrey Show* the month it is released.

Mid-1950s: Top-selling Little Golden Books center on children's TV shows and Westerns (*The Roy Rogers Show, Howdy Doody, The Lone Ranger, Captain Kangaroo,* etc.).

Early 1960s: A large number of new Little Golden Books focus on popular Saturday-morning TV shows, such as *Huckleberry Hound, The Bullwinkle Show, Yogi Bear, The Flintstones,* and *Bozo the Clown.*

> **LITTLE GOLDEN BOOKS**
> ❋ **1980s–1990s** ❋
> **AVERAGE COST:**
> **89¢ (1982)**
> **99¢ (1986)**

1982: Little Golden Books turns 40. More than 800 million books have been sold.

November 20, 1986: The one billionth Little Golden Book (*The Poky Little Puppy*) is printed.

1992: Little Golden Books celebrates its golden anniversary. In recognition of this milestone, a permanent collection of Little Golden Books and artwork is given to the Smithsonian Institution's Division of Cultural History.

> **LITTLE GOLDEN BOOKS**
> ❀ **TODAY** ❀
> **AVERAGE COST: $2.99**

February 2001: The Little Golden Book Classic line is launched with great success. This new line revives vintage Little Golden Books found in the archives. The first six in this new library are:

Richard Scarry's Good Night, Little Bear
Animal Orchestra
The Lion's Paw
The Fire Engine Book
The Little Red Hen
The Good Humor® Man

March 2001: The Little Golden Book Classic line wins a 2001 Dr. Toy "Best Classic Toy" Award.

March 2001: *Publishers Weekly* lists *Scooby-Doo: The Haunted Carnival* as the third bestselling hardcover children's book of 2000.

December 2001: *Publishers Weekly* lists *The Poky Little Puppy* as the bestselling children's book of all time.

January 2002: Golden Books kicks off its sixtieth anniversary year with a special-edition boxed set of Little Golden Book Classics. The Golden Books library now includes more than 1,200 titles!

October 1, 2002: Happy sixtieth birthday, Little Golden Books!

2002: To date, more than 2 billion Little Golden Books have been printed. Stacked on top of each other, they would reach the moon!

Much of the historical information here was taken from *Collecting Little Golden Books®: A Collector's Identification and Price Guide,* by Steve Santi (Krause Publications).